AR 2.5 BL

AR 0.5 PTS

Here comes Spider-Man /

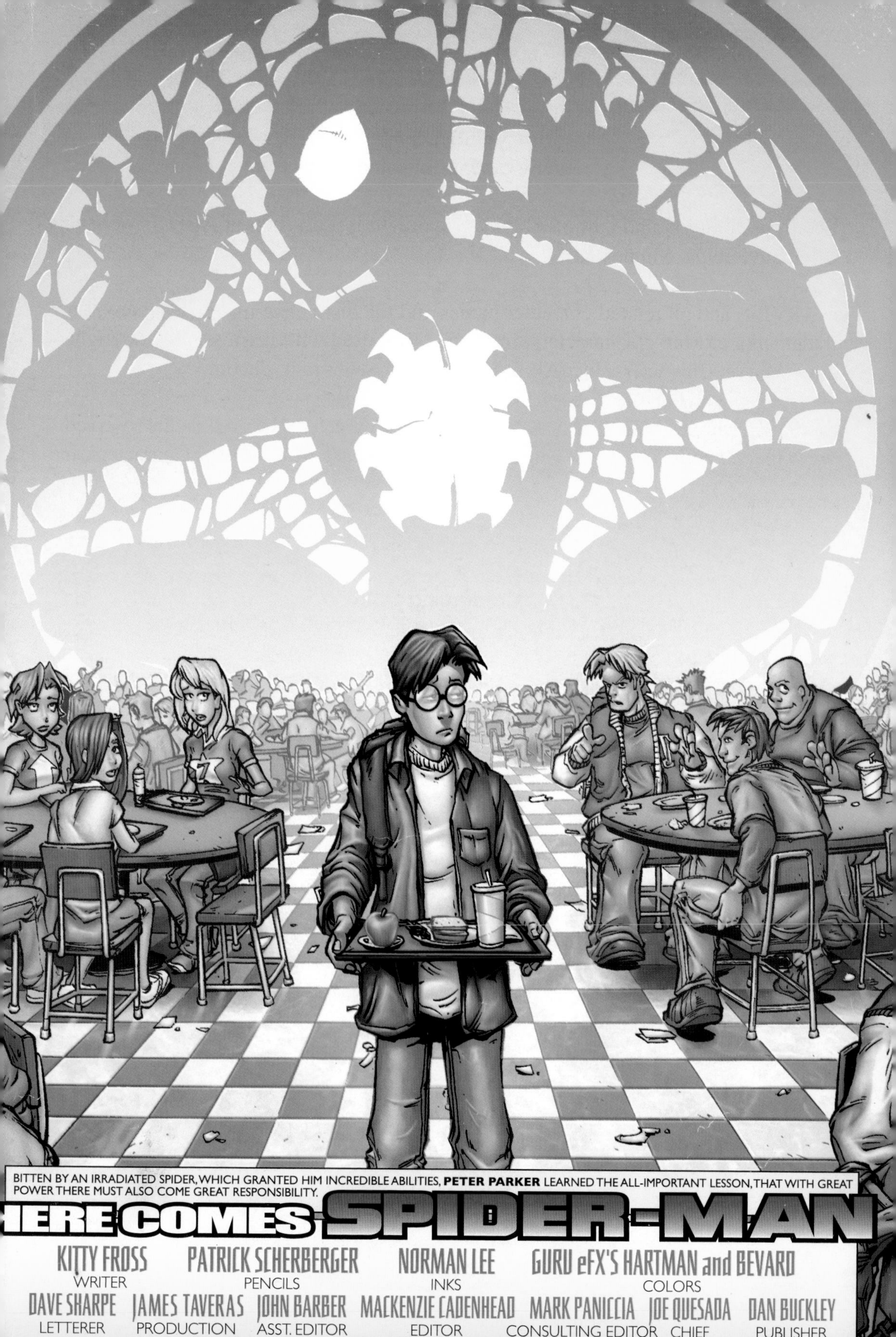

BITTEN BY AN IRRADIATED SPIDER, WHICH GRANTED HIM INCREDIBLE ABILITIES, **PETER PARKER** LEARNED THE ALL-IMPORTANT LESSON, THAT WITH GREAT POWER THERE MUST ALSO COME GREAT RESPONSIBILITY.

HERE COMES SPIDER-MAN

KITTY FROSS — WRITER
PATRICK SCHERBERGER — PENCILS
NORMAN LEE — INKS
GURU eFX'S HARTMAN and BEVARD — COLORS
DAVE SHARPE — LETTERER
JAMES TAVERAS — PRODUCTION
JOHN BARBER — ASST. EDITOR
MACKENZIE CADENHEAD — EDITOR
MARK PANICCIA — CONSULTING EDITOR
JOE QUESADA — CHIEF
DAN BUCKLEY — PUBLISHER

Adapted from AMAZING FANTASY #15 by STAN LEE and STEVE DITKO

MARVEL
Spotlight

VISIT US AT
www.abdopublishing.com

Spotlight library bound edition © 2007. Spotlight is a division of ABDO Publishing Company, Edina, Minnesota.

Cataloging Data

Fross, Kitty
    Here comes Spider-Man / Kitty Fross, writer ; Patrick Scherberger, pencils ; Norman Lee, inks -- Library bound ed.
        p. cm. -- (Spider-Man)
    Summary: Introduces readers of all ages to some of the greatest stories of the legendary Marvel Universe.
    "Marvel age"--Cover.
    Revision of the May 2005 issue Marvel adventures Spider-Man.
    ISBN-13: 978-1-59961-210-2 (Reinforced Library Bound Edition)
    ISBN-10: 1-59961-210-0 (Reinforced Library Bound Edition)
    1. Spider-Man (Fictitious character)--Fiction. 2. Comic books, strips, etc.--Fiction. 3. Graphic novels. I. Title. II. Series.

741.5dc22

All Spotlight books are reinforced library binding and manufactured in the United States of America

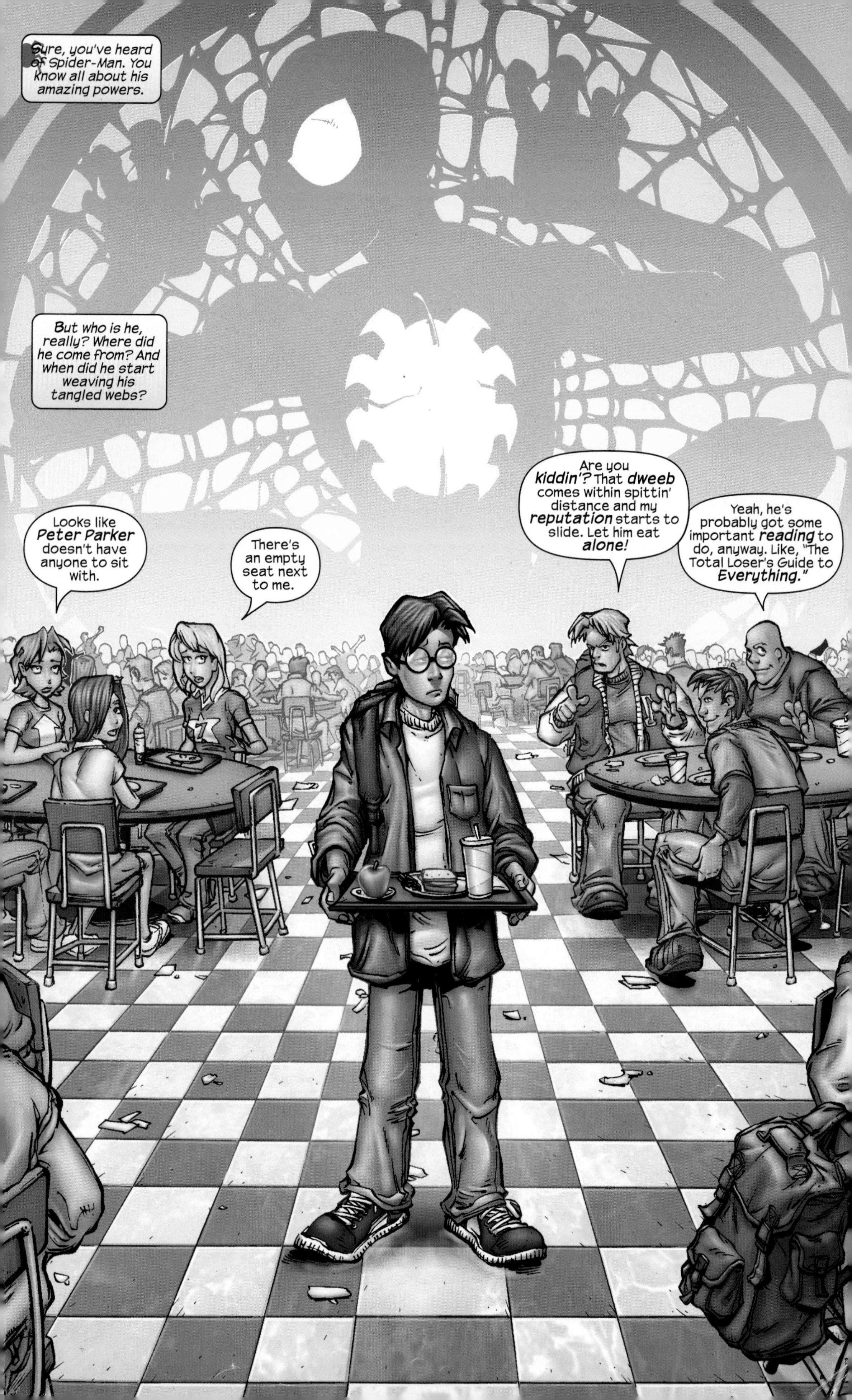
Sure, you've heard of Spider-Man. You know all about his amazing powers.
But who is he, really? Where did he come from? And when did he start weaving his tangled webs?
Looks like Peter Parker doesn't have anyone to sit with.
There's an empty seat next to me.
Are you kiddin'? That dweeb comes within spittin' distance and my reputation starts to slide. Let him eat alone!
Yeah, he's probably got some important reading to do, anyway. Like, "The Total Loser's Guide to Everything."

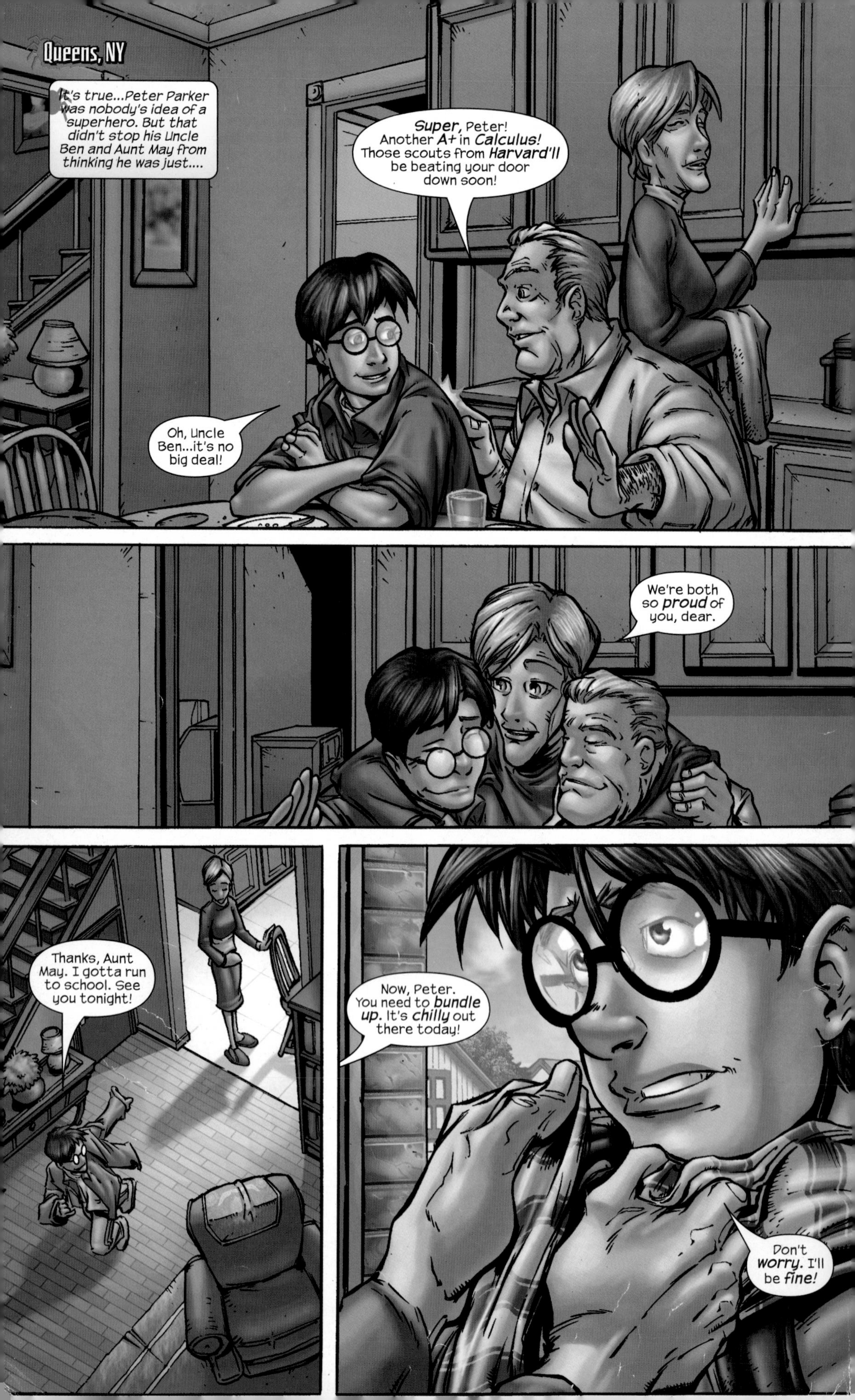
Queens, NY
It's true...Peter Parker was nobody's idea of a superhero. But that didn't stop his Uncle Ben and Aunt May from thinking he was just....
Super, Peter! Another A+ in Calculus! Those scouts from Harvard'll be beating your door down soon!
Oh, Uncle Ben...it's no big deal!
We're both so proud of you, dear.
Thanks, Aunt May. I gotta run to school. See you tonight!
Now, Peter. You need to bundle up. It's chilly out there today!
Don't worry. I'll be fine!

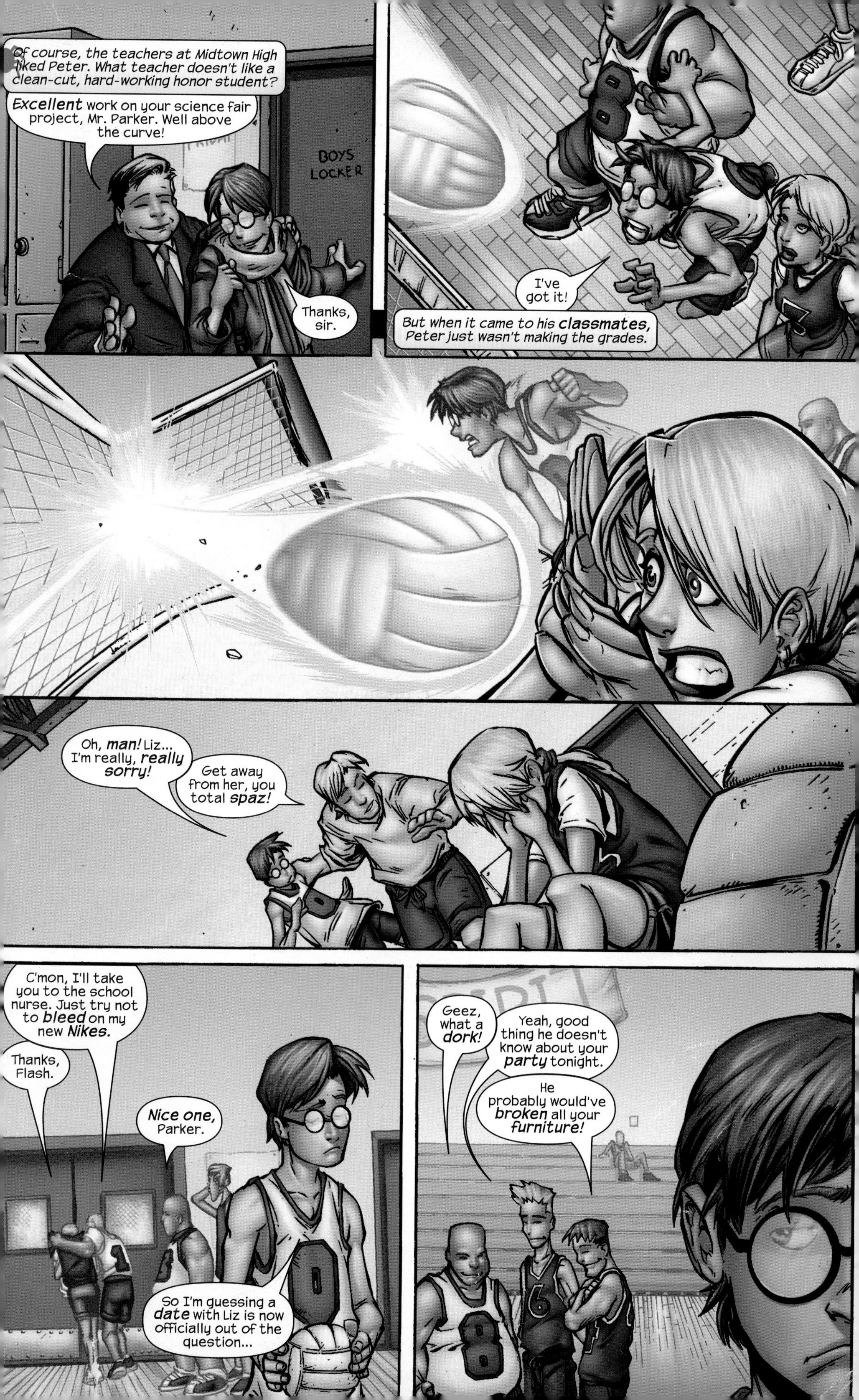
Of course, the teachers at Midtown High liked Peter. What teacher doesn't like a clean-cut, hard-working honor student?
Excellent work on your science fair project, Mr. Parker. Well above the curve!
BOYS LOCKER
Thanks, sir.
I've got it!
But when it came to his classmates, Peter just wasn't making the grades.
Oh, man! Liz... I'm really, really sorry!
Get away from her, you total spaz!
C'mon, I'll take you to the school nurse. Just try not to bleed on my new Nikes.
Thanks, Flash.
Nice one, Parker.
So I'm guessing a date with Liz is now officially out of the question...
Geez, what a dork!
Yeah, good thing he doesn't know about your party tonight.
He probably would've broken all your furniture!

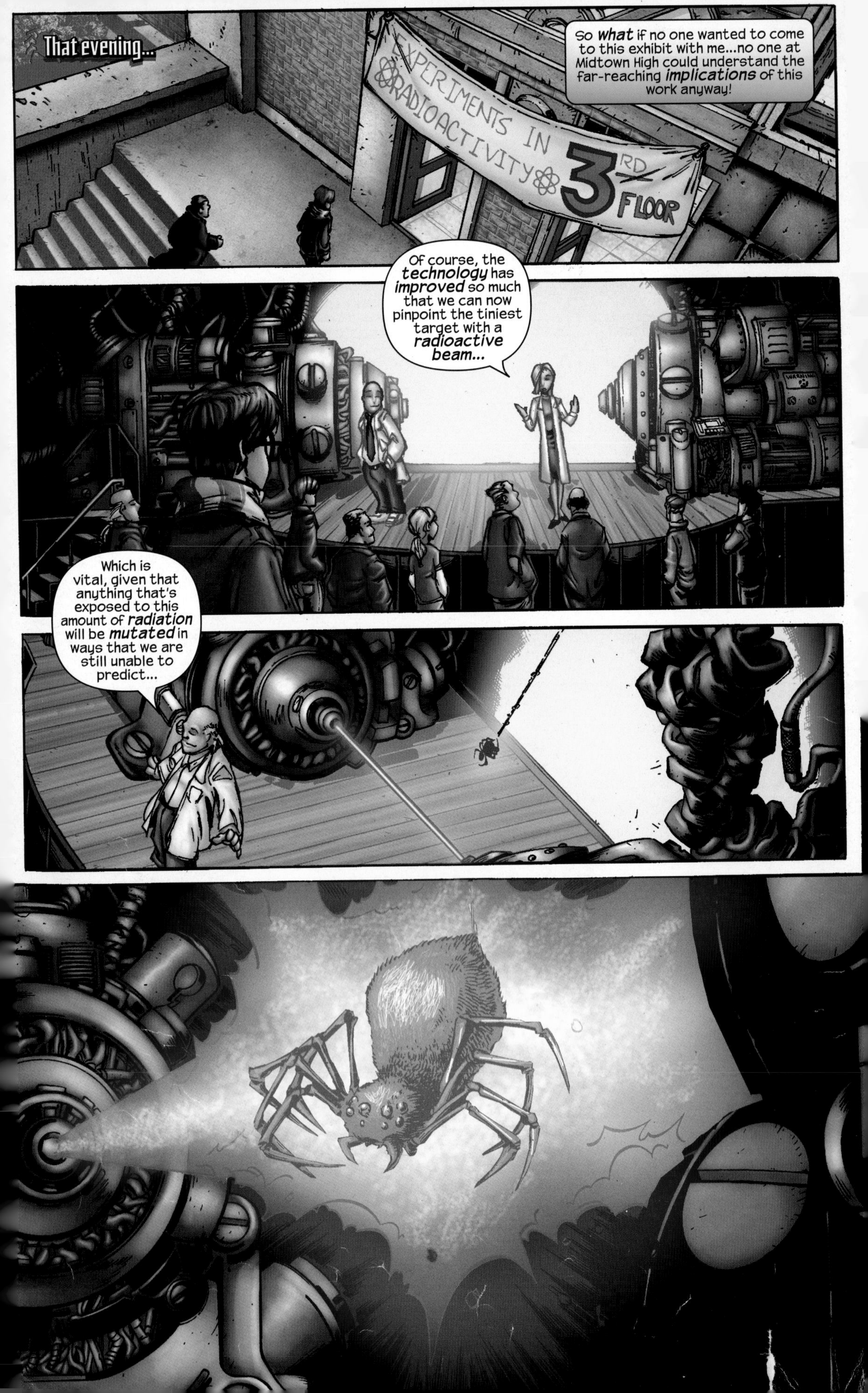

That evening...
So what if no one wanted to come to this exhibit with me...no one at Midtown High could understand the far-reaching implications of this work anyway!
EXPERIMENTS IN RADIOACTIVITY 3RD FLOOR
Of course, the technology has improved so much that we can now pinpoint the tiniest target with a radioactive beam...
Which is vital, given that anything that's exposed to this amount of radiation will be mutated in ways that we are still unable to predict...

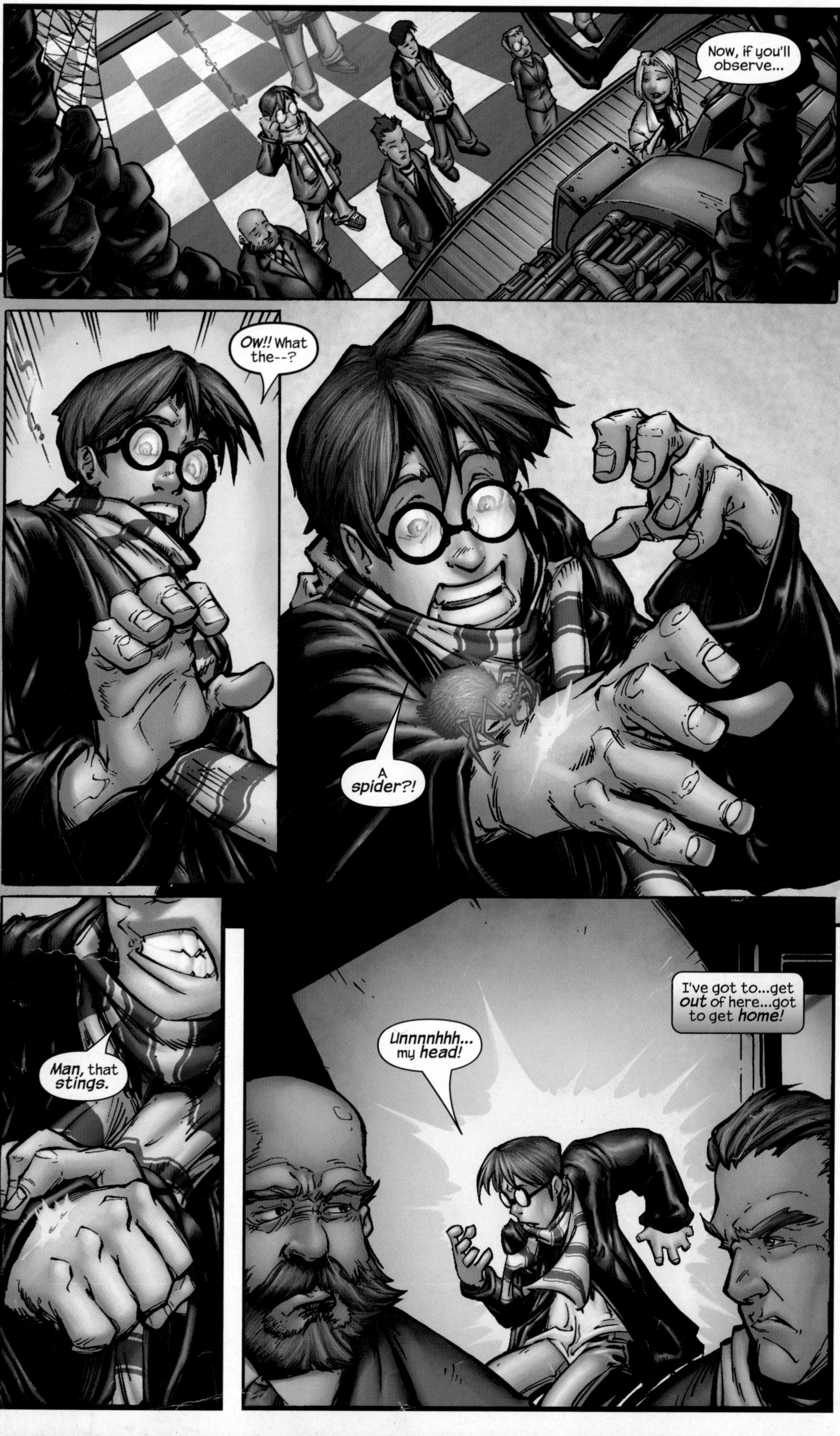
Now, if you'll observe...
Ow!! What the--?
A spider?!
Man, that stings.
Unnnnhhh... my head!
I've got to...get out of here...got to get home!

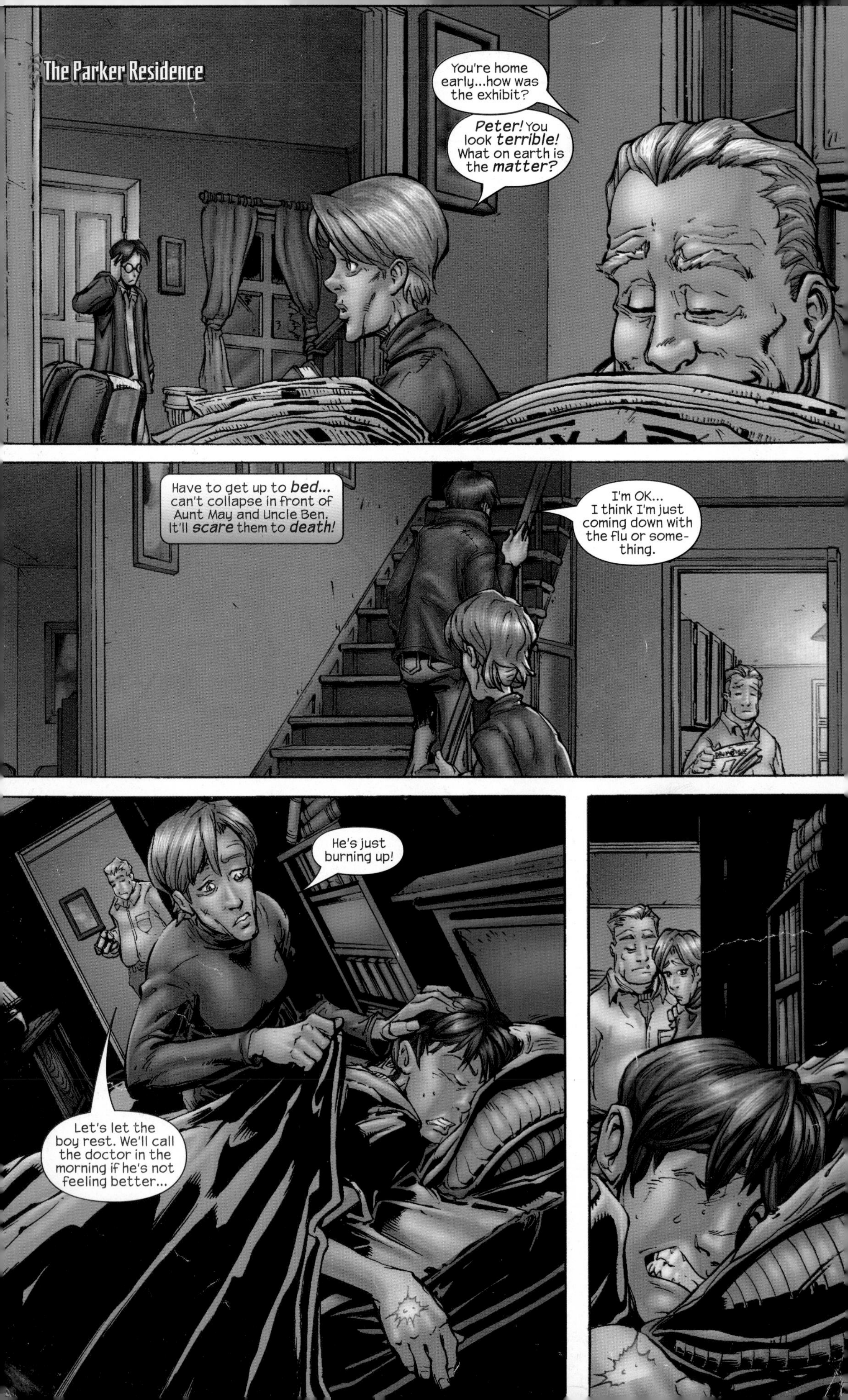

The Parker Residence
You're home early...how was the exhibit?
Peter! You look terrible! What on earth is the matter?
Have to get up to bed... can't collapse in front of Aunt May and Uncle Ben. It'll scare them to death!
I'm OK... I think I'm just coming down with the flu or some-thing.
He's just burning up!
Let's let the boy rest. We'll call the doctor in the morning if he's not feeling better...

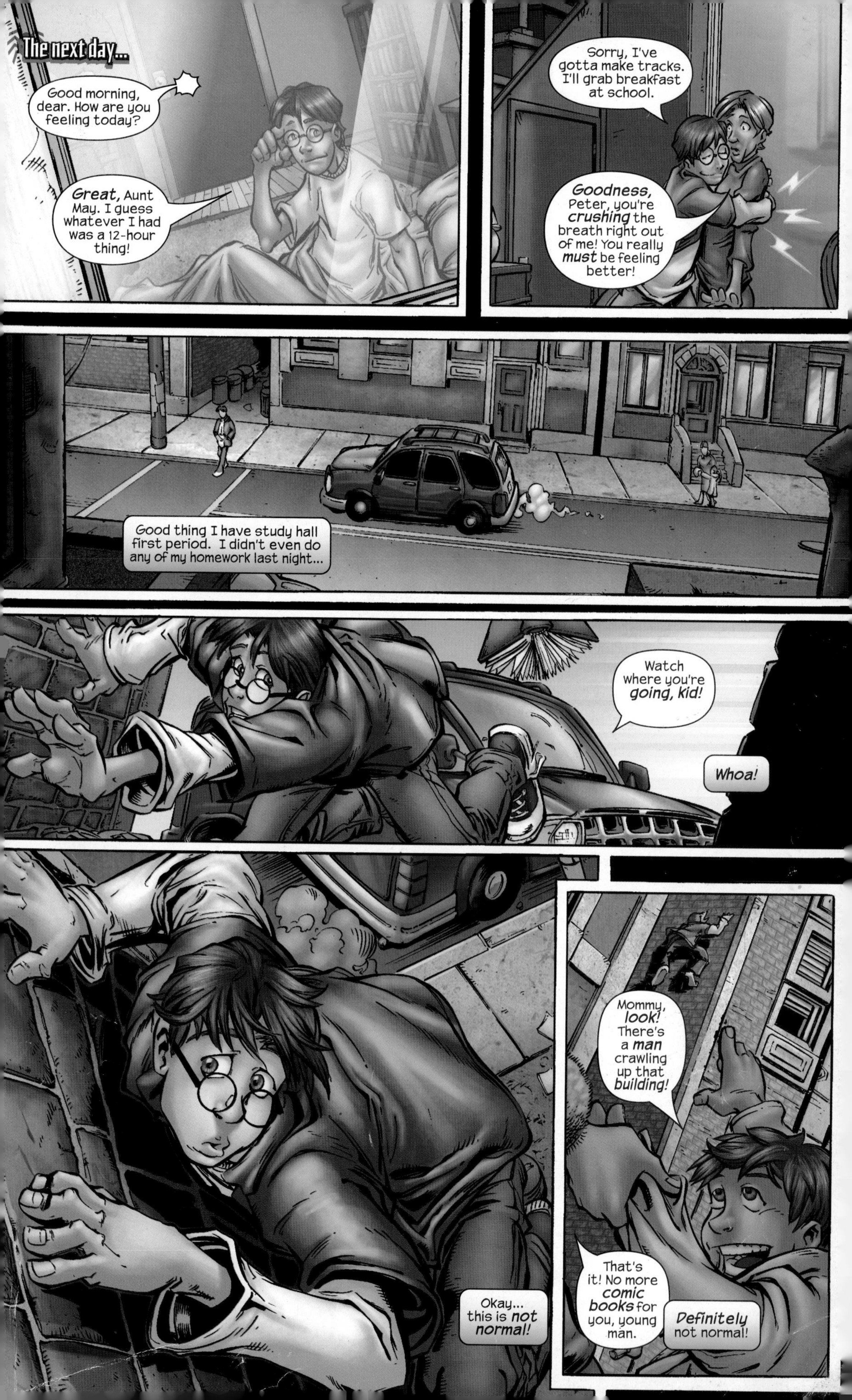

The next day...
Good morning, dear. How are you feeling today?
Great, Aunt May. I guess whatever I had was a 12-hour thing!
Sorry, I've gotta make tracks. I'll grab breakfast at school.
Goodness, Peter, you're crushing the breath right out of me! You really must be feeling better!
Good thing I have study hall first period. I didn't even do any of my homework last night...
Watch where you're going, kid!
Whoa!
Okay... this is not normal!
Mommy, look! There's a man crawling up that building!
That's it! No more comic books for you, young man.
Definitely not normal!

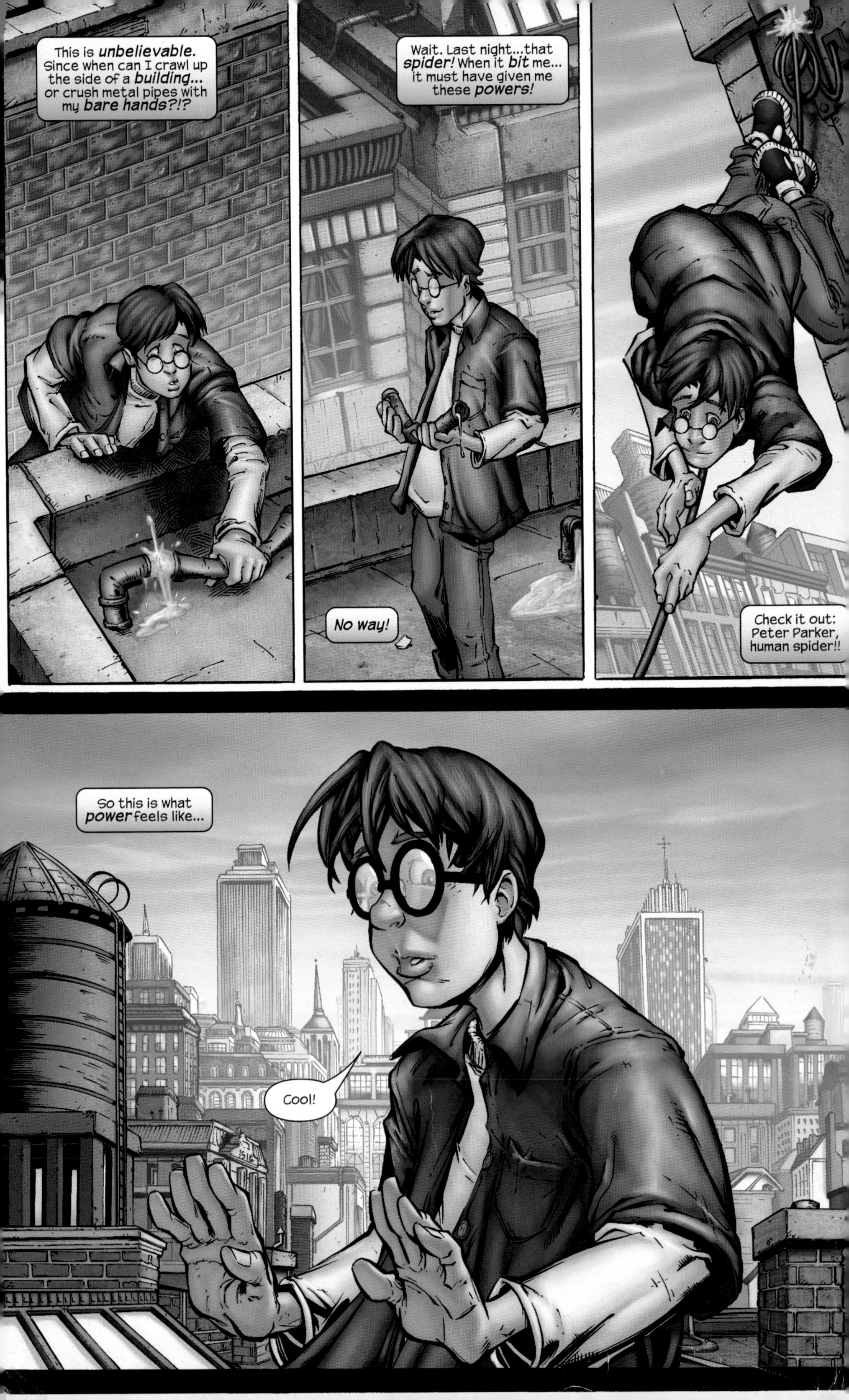
This is unbelievable. Since when can I crawl up the side of a building... or crush metal pipes with my bare hands?!?
Wait. Last night...that spider! When it bit me... it must have given me these powers!
No way!
Check it out: Peter Parker, human spider!!
So this is what power feels like...
Cool!

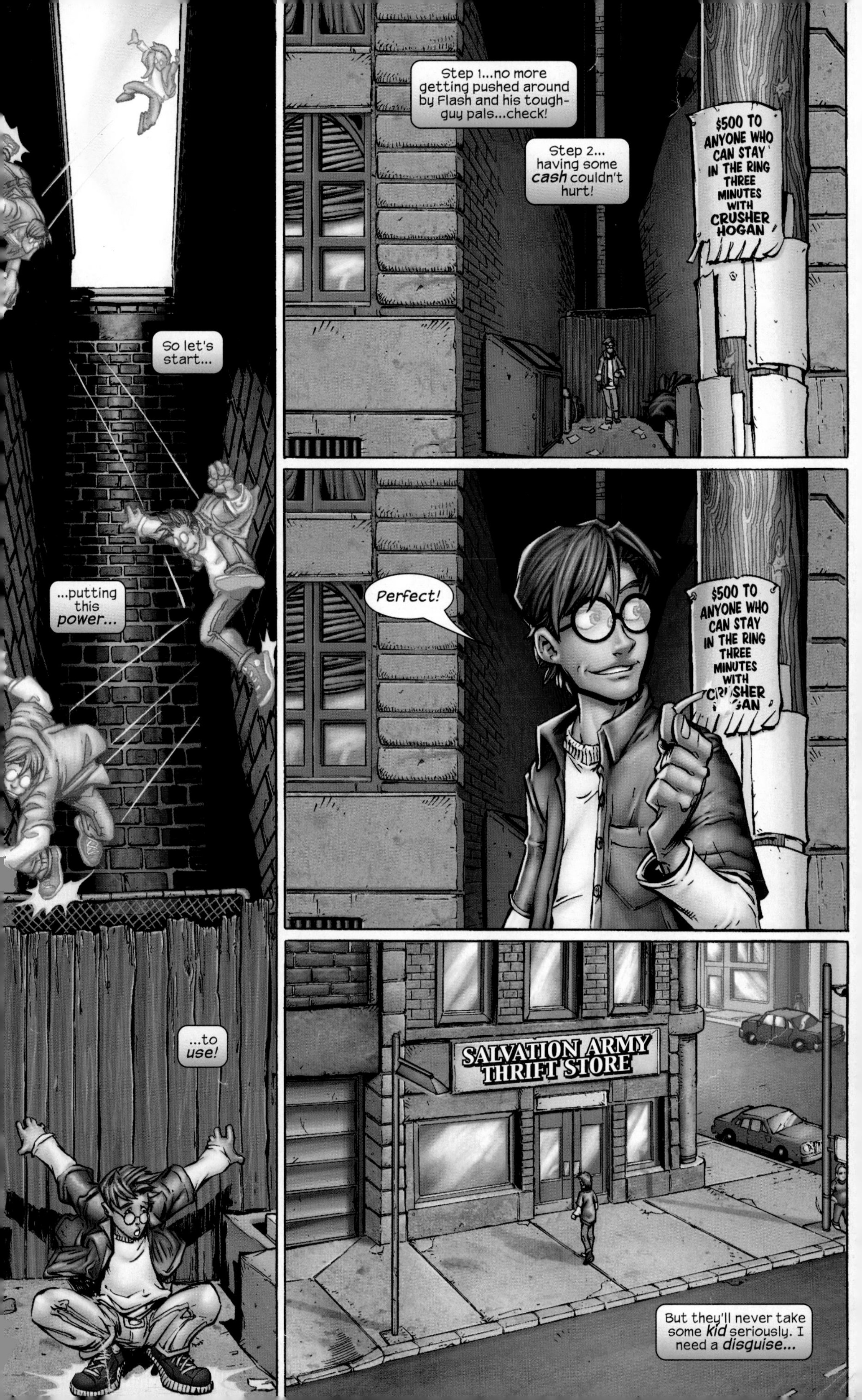
So let's start...
...putting this power...
...to use!
Step 1...no more getting pushed around by Flash and his tough-guy pals...check!
Step 2... having some cash couldn't hurt!
$500 TO ANYONE WHO CAN STAY IN THE RING THREE MINUTES WITH CRUSHER HOGAN
Perfect!
SALVATION ARMY THRIFT STORE
But they'll never take some kid seriously. I need a disguise...

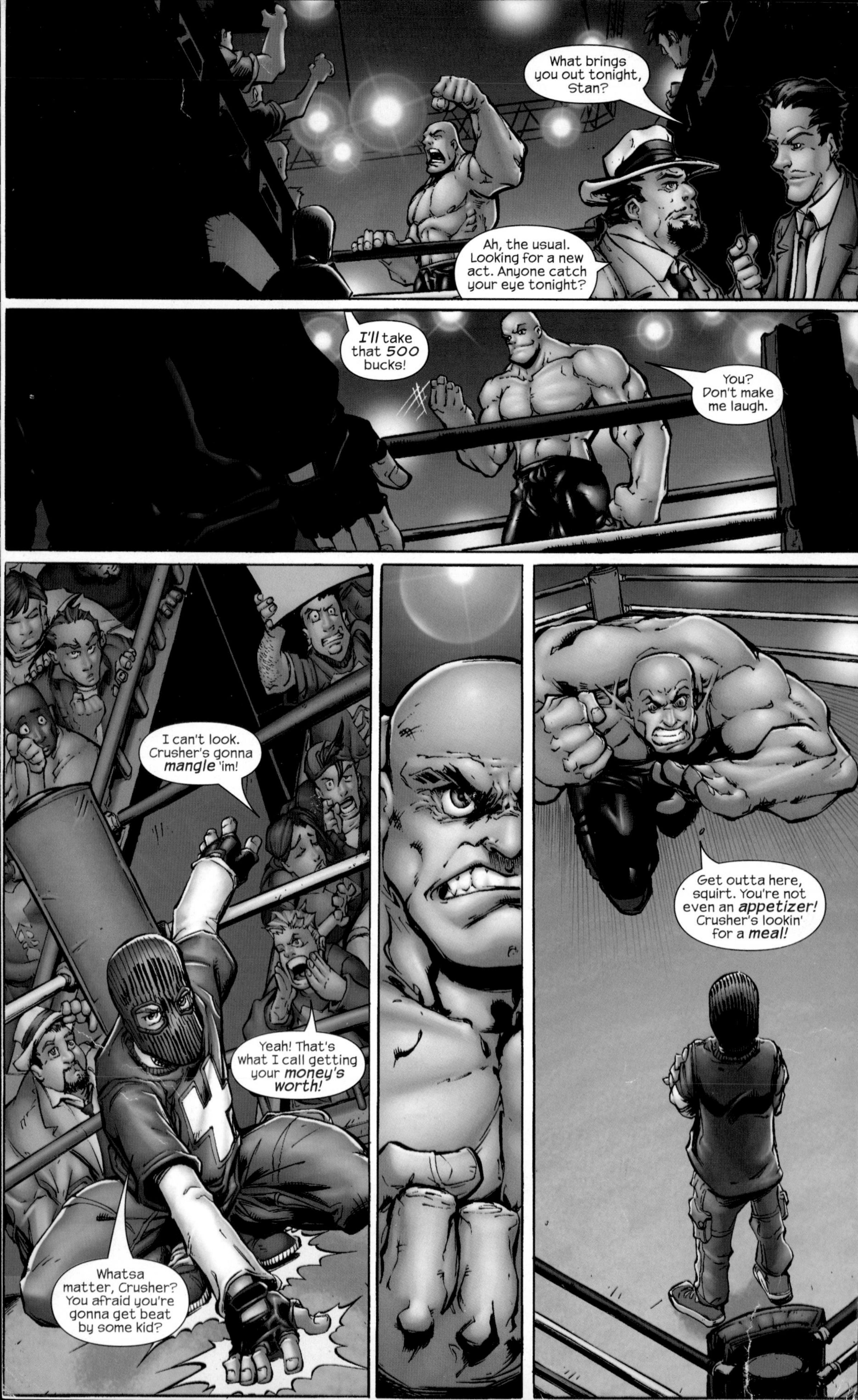

What brings you out tonight, Stan?
Ah, the usual. Looking for a new act. Anyone catch your eye tonight?
I'll take that 500 bucks!
You? Don't make me laugh.
I can't look. Crusher's gonna mangle 'im!
Yeah! That's what I call getting your money's worth!
Whatsa matter, Crusher? You afraid you're gonna get beat by some kid?
Get outta here, squirt. You're not even an appetizer! Crusher's lookin' for a meal!

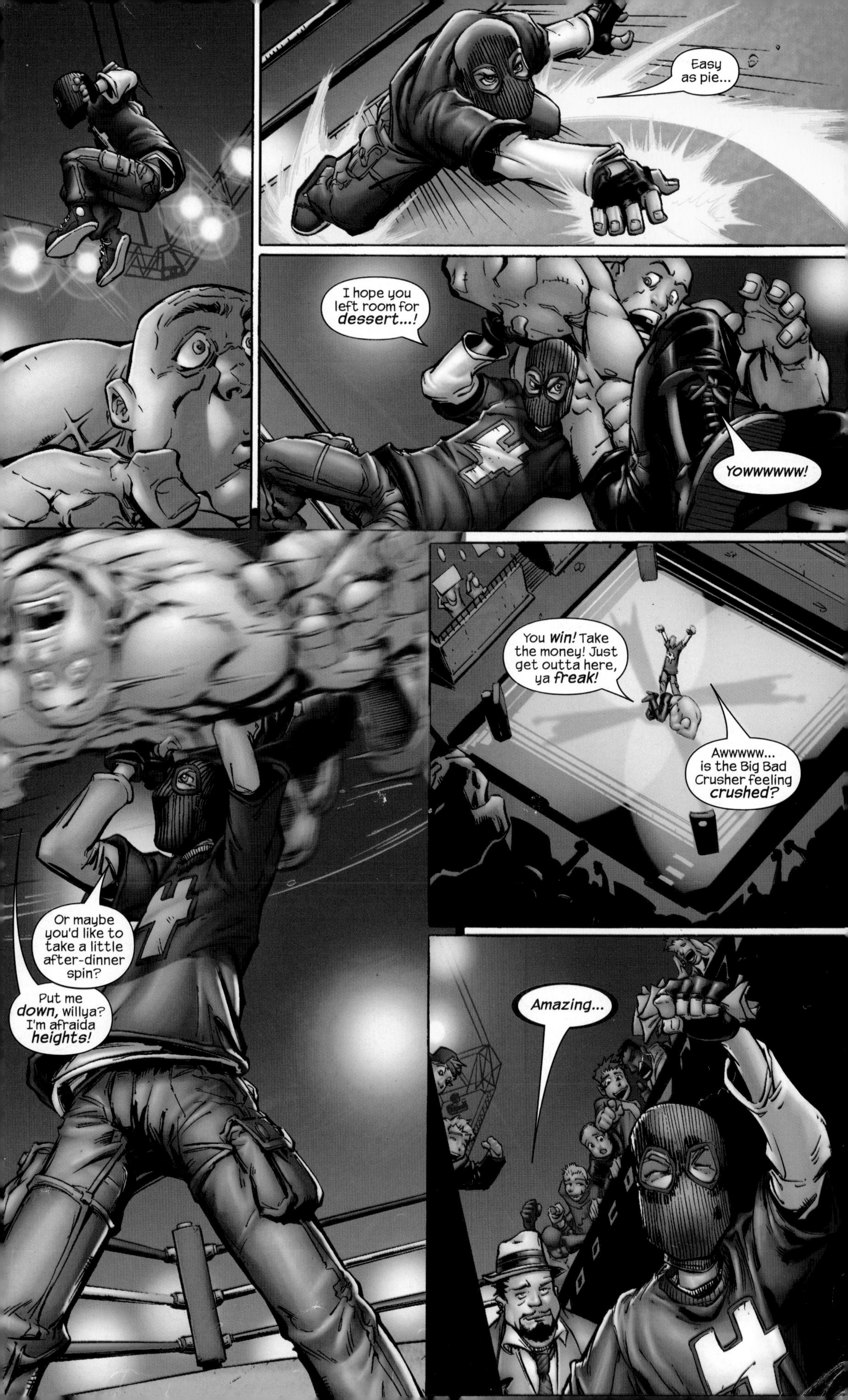
Easy as pie...
I hope you left room for dessert...!
YOWWWWWW!
Or maybe you'd like to take a little after-dinner spin?
Put me down, willya? I'm afraida heights!
You win! Take the money! Just get outta here, ya freak!
Awwwww... is the Big Bad Crusher feeling crushed?
Amazing...

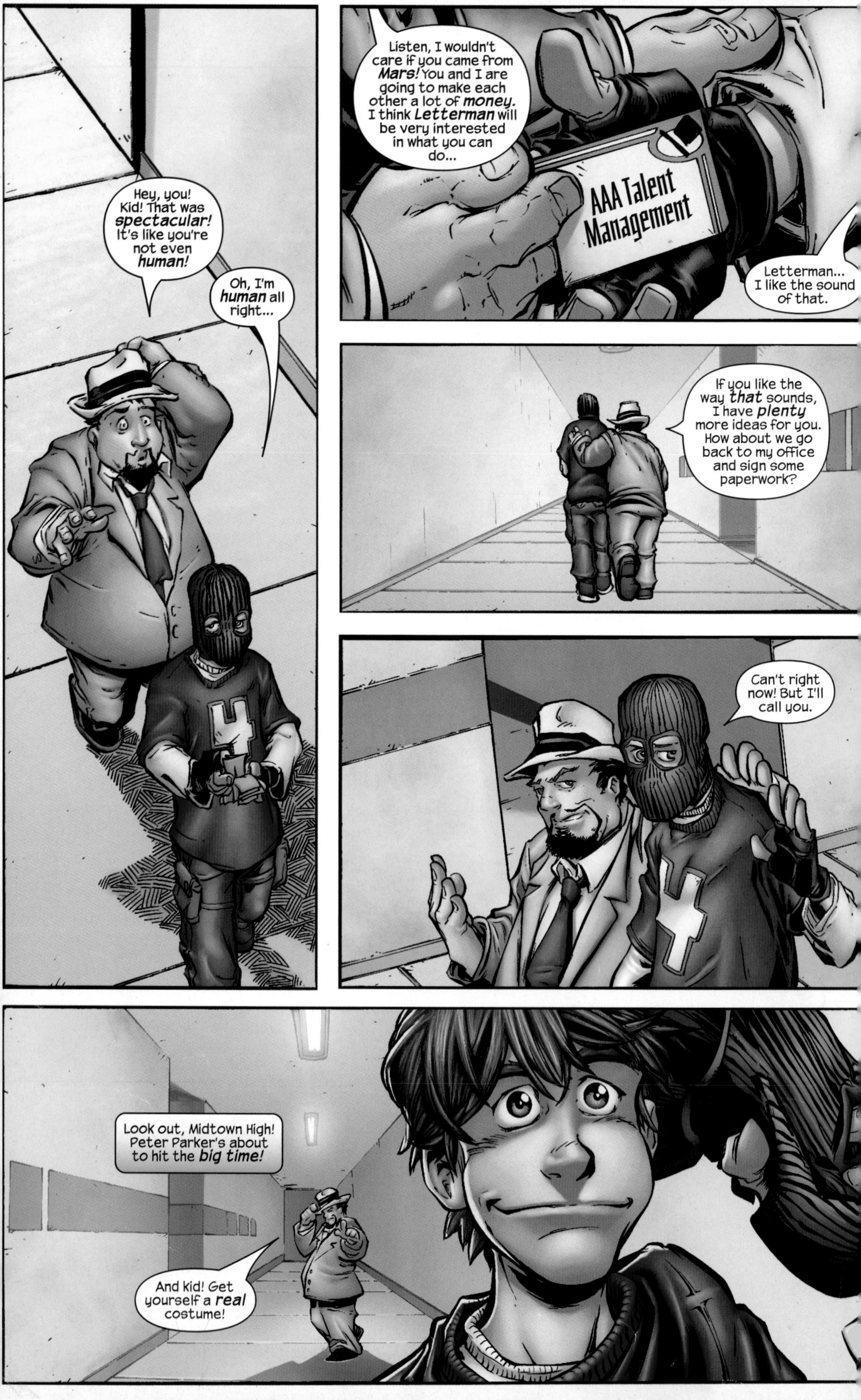
Hey, you! Kid! That was spectacular! It's like you're not even human!
Oh, I'm human all right...
Listen, I wouldn't care if you came from Mars! You and I are going to make each other a lot of money. I think Letterman will be very interested in what you can do...
AAA Talent Management
Letterman... I like the sound of that.
If you like the way that sounds, I have plenty more ideas for you. How about we go back to my office and sign some paperwork?
Can't right now! But I'll call you.
Look out, Midtown High! Peter Parker's about to hit the big time!
And kid! Get yourself a real costume!

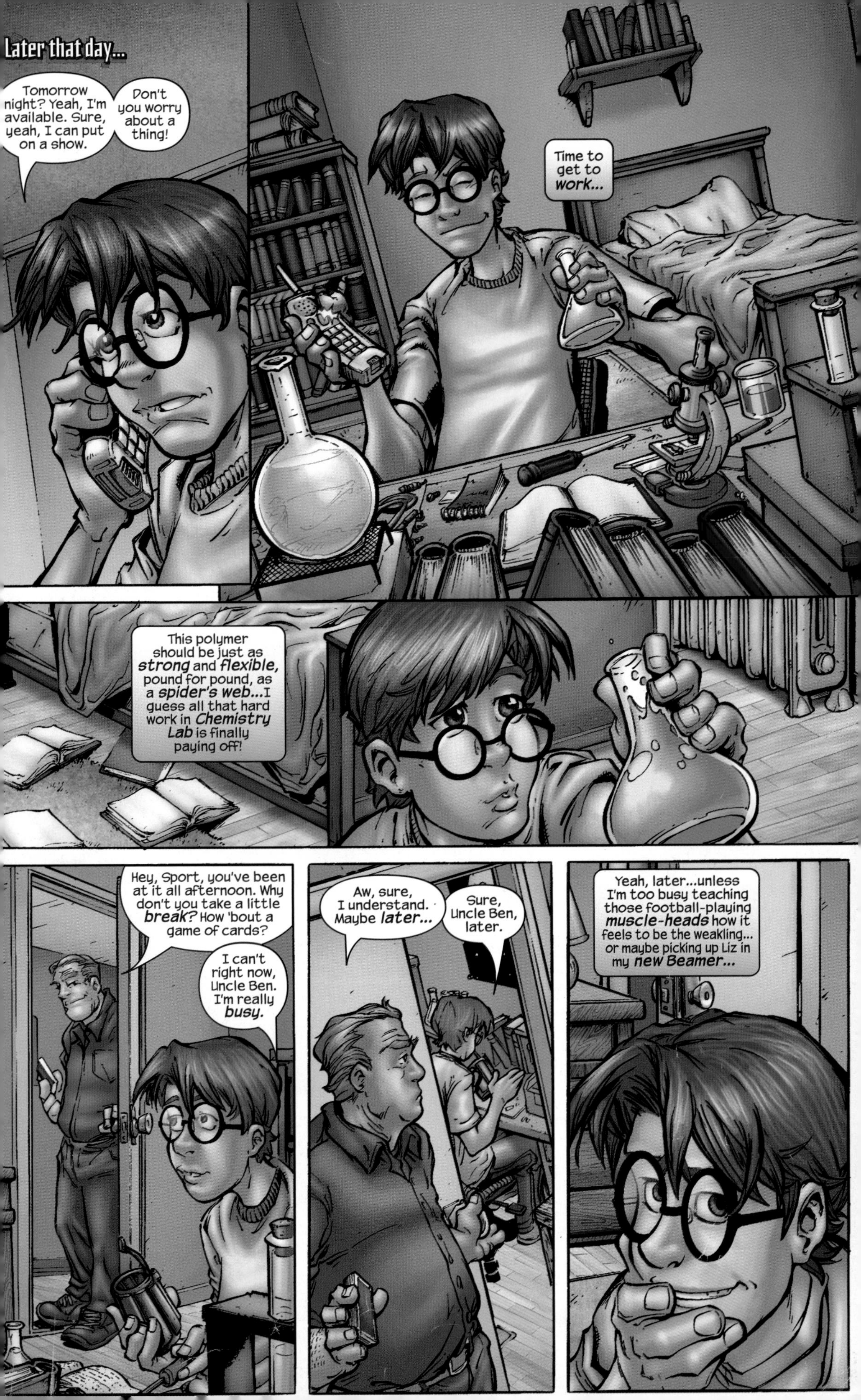
Later that day...
Tomorrow night? Yeah, I'm available. Sure, yeah, I can put on a show.
Don't you worry about a thing!
Time to get to work...
This polymer should be just as strong and flexible, pound for pound, as a spider's web...I guess all that hard work in Chemistry Lab is finally paying off!
Hey, Sport, you've been at it all afternoon. Why don't you take a little break? How 'bout a game of cards?
I can't right now, Uncle Ben. I'm really busy.
Aw, sure, I understand. Maybe later...
Sure, Uncle Ben, later.
Yeah, later...unless I'm too busy teaching those football-playing muscle-heads how it feels to be the weakling... or maybe picking up Liz in my new Beamer...

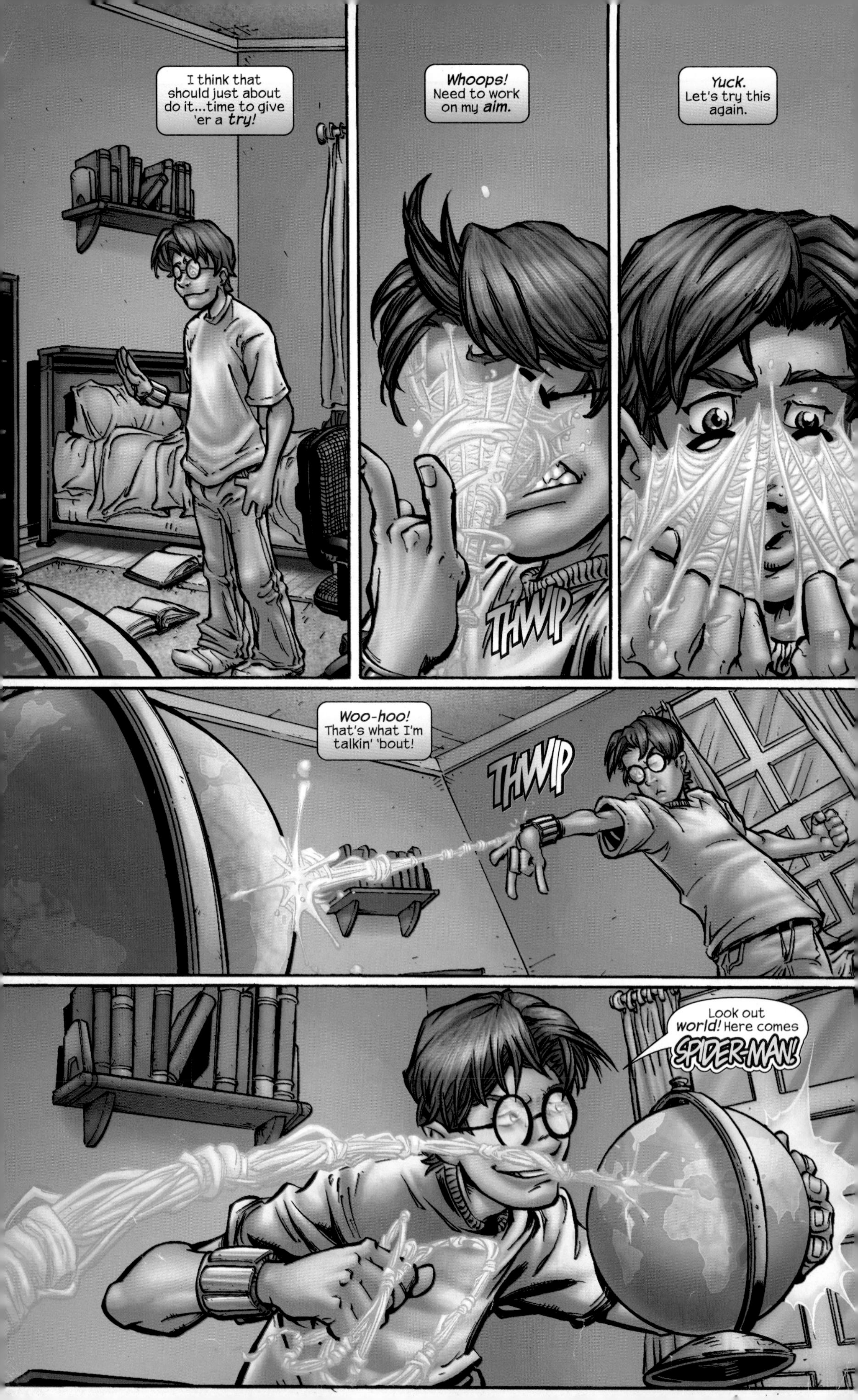
I think that should just about do it...time to give 'er a try!
Whoops! Need to work on my aim.
THWIP
Yuck. Let's try this again.
Woo-hoo! That's what I'm talkin' 'bout!
THWIP
Look out world! Here comes SPIDER-MAN!

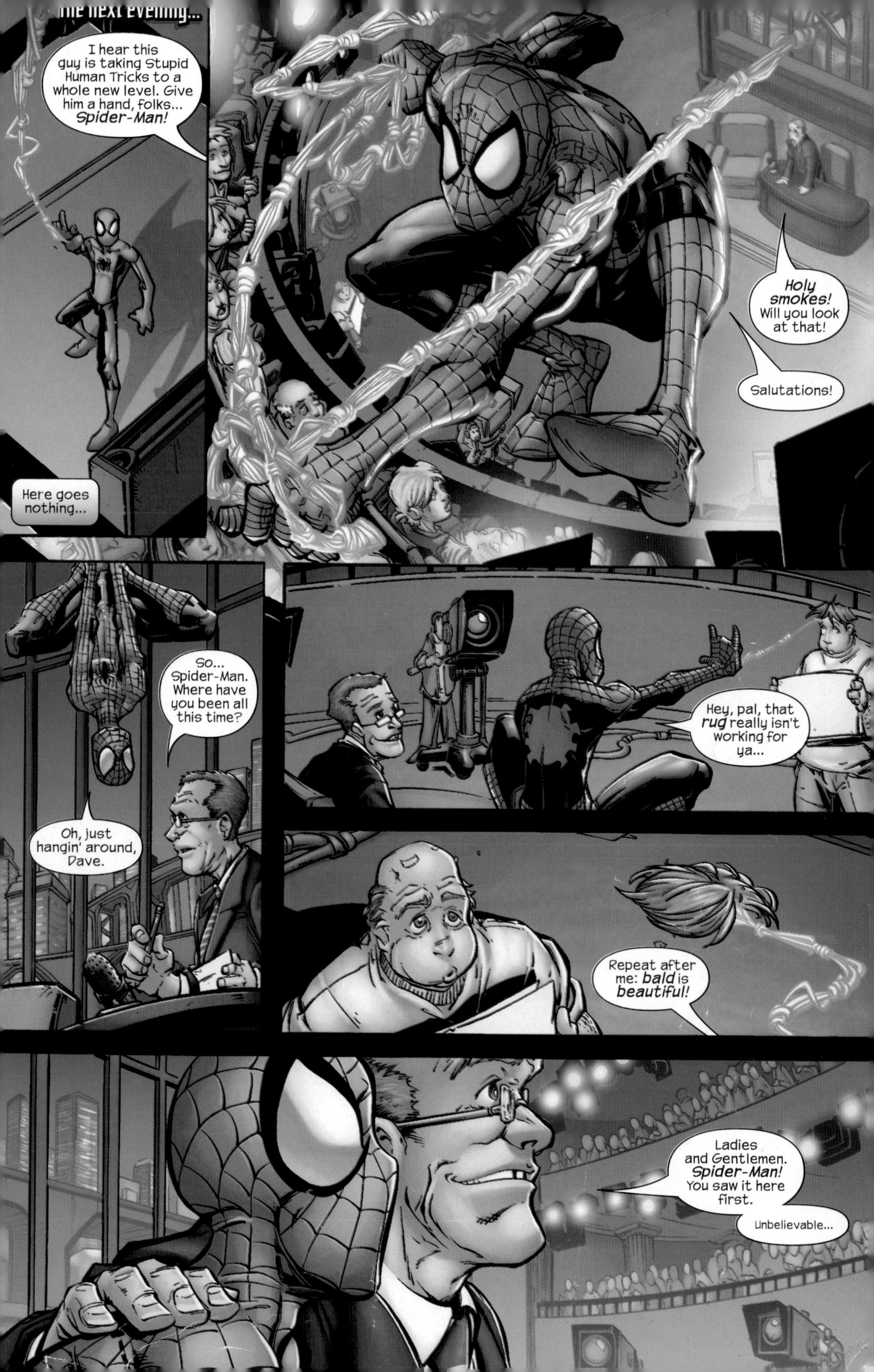
The next evening...
I hear this guy is taking Stupid Human Tricks to a whole new level. Give him a hand, folks... Spider-Man!
Here goes nothing...
Holy smokes! Will you look at that!
Salutations!
So... Spider-Man. Where have you been all this time?
Oh, just hangin' around, Dave.
Hey, pal, that rug really isn't working for ya...
Repeat after me: bald is beautiful!
Ladies and Gentlemen. Spider-Man! You saw it here first.
Unbelievable...

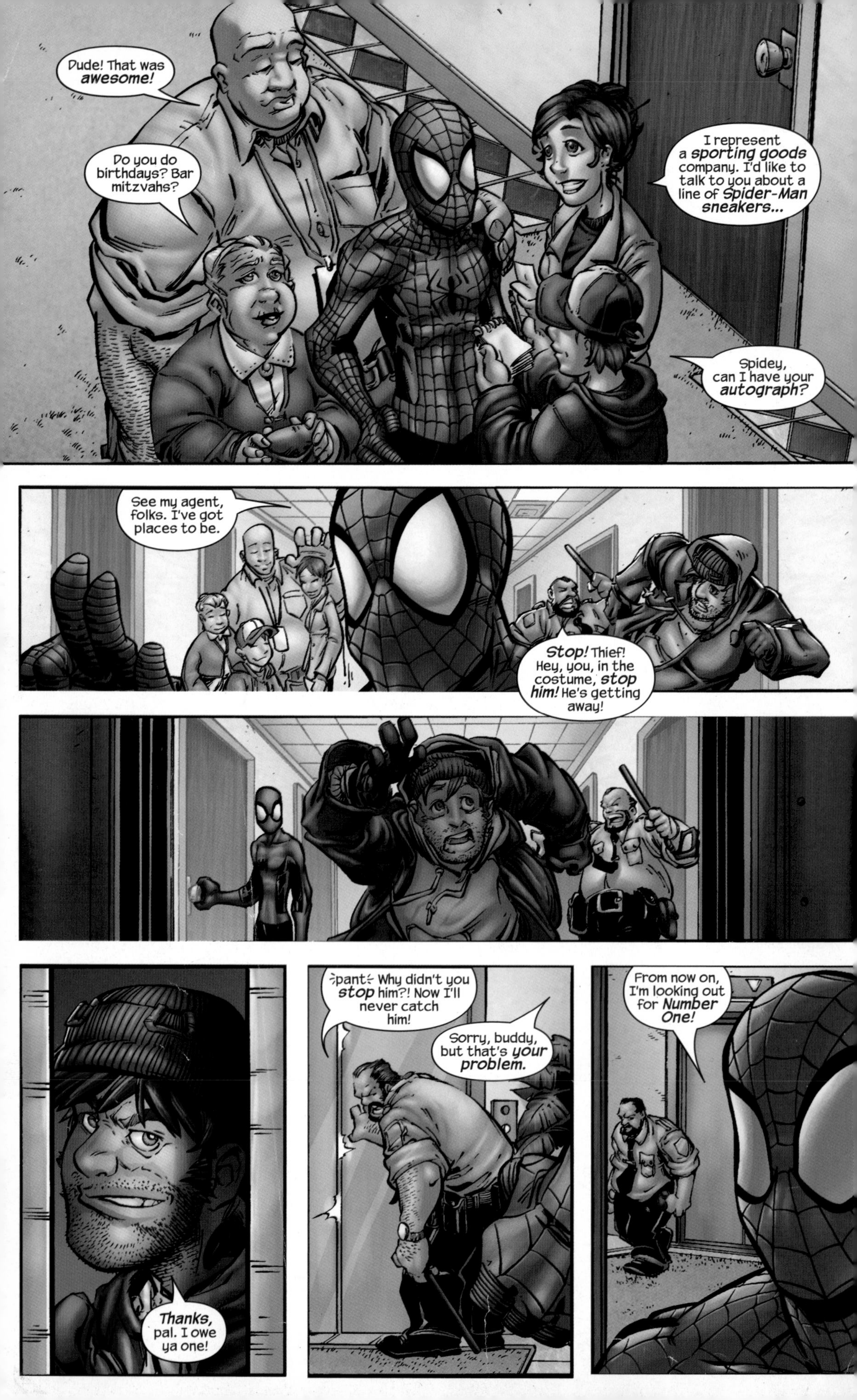
Dude! That was awesome!
Do you do birthdays? Bar mitzvahs?
I represent a sporting goods company. I'd like to talk to you about a line of Spider-Man sneakers...
Spidey, can I have your autograph?
See my agent, folks. I've got places to be.
Stop! Thief! Hey, you, in the costume, stop him! He's getting away!
Thanks, pal. I owe ya one!
pant Why didn't you stop him?! Now I'll never catch him!
Sorry, buddy, but that's your problem.
From now on, I'm looking out for Number One!

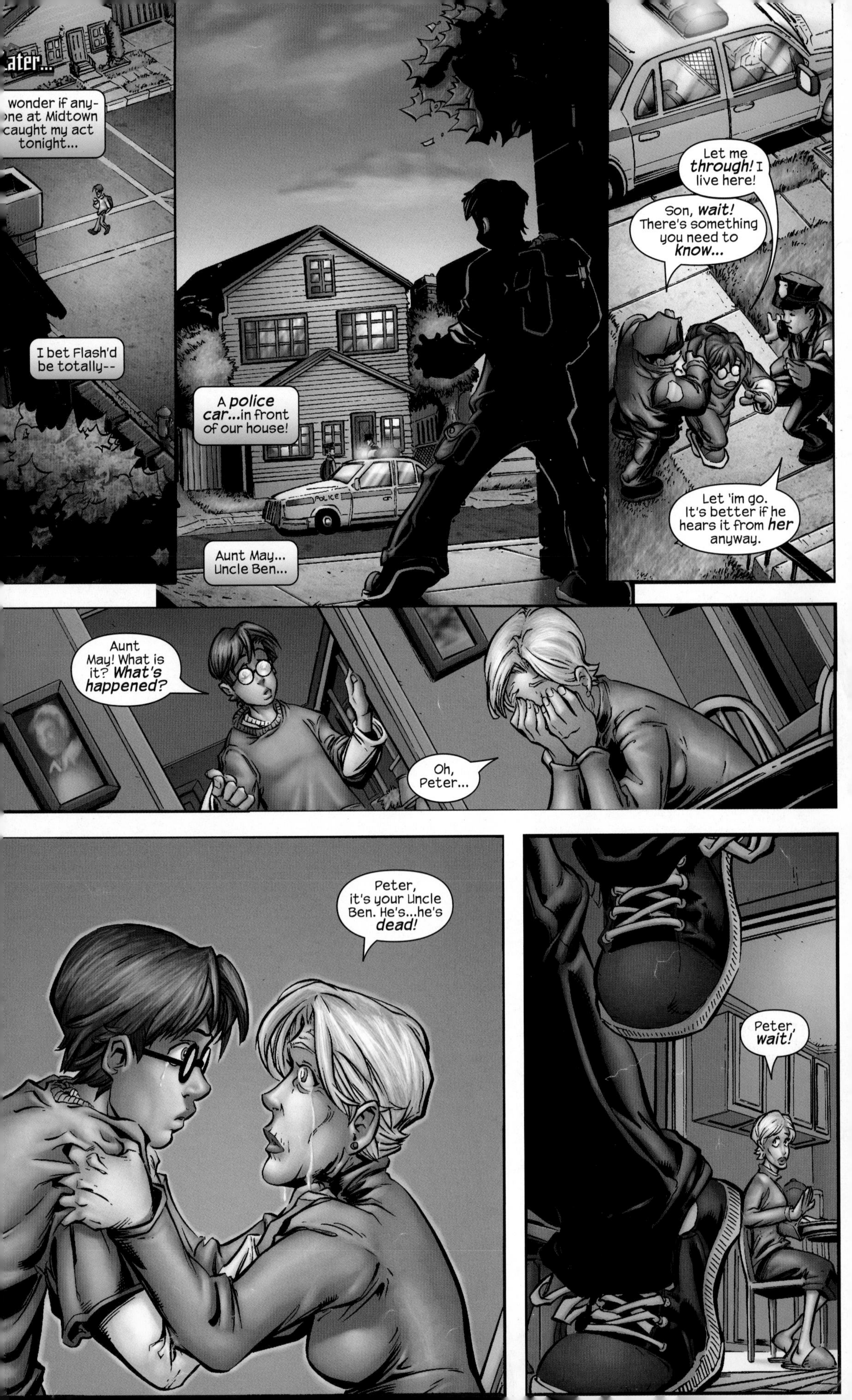
Later...
I wonder if anyone at Midtown caught my act tonight...
I bet Flash'd be totally--
A police car...in front of our house!
Aunt May... Uncle Ben...
Let me through! I live here!
Son, wait! There's something you need to know...
Let 'im go. It's better if he hears it from her anyway.
Aunt May! What is it? What's happened?
Oh, Peter...
Peter, it's your Uncle Ben. He's...he's dead!
Peter, wait!

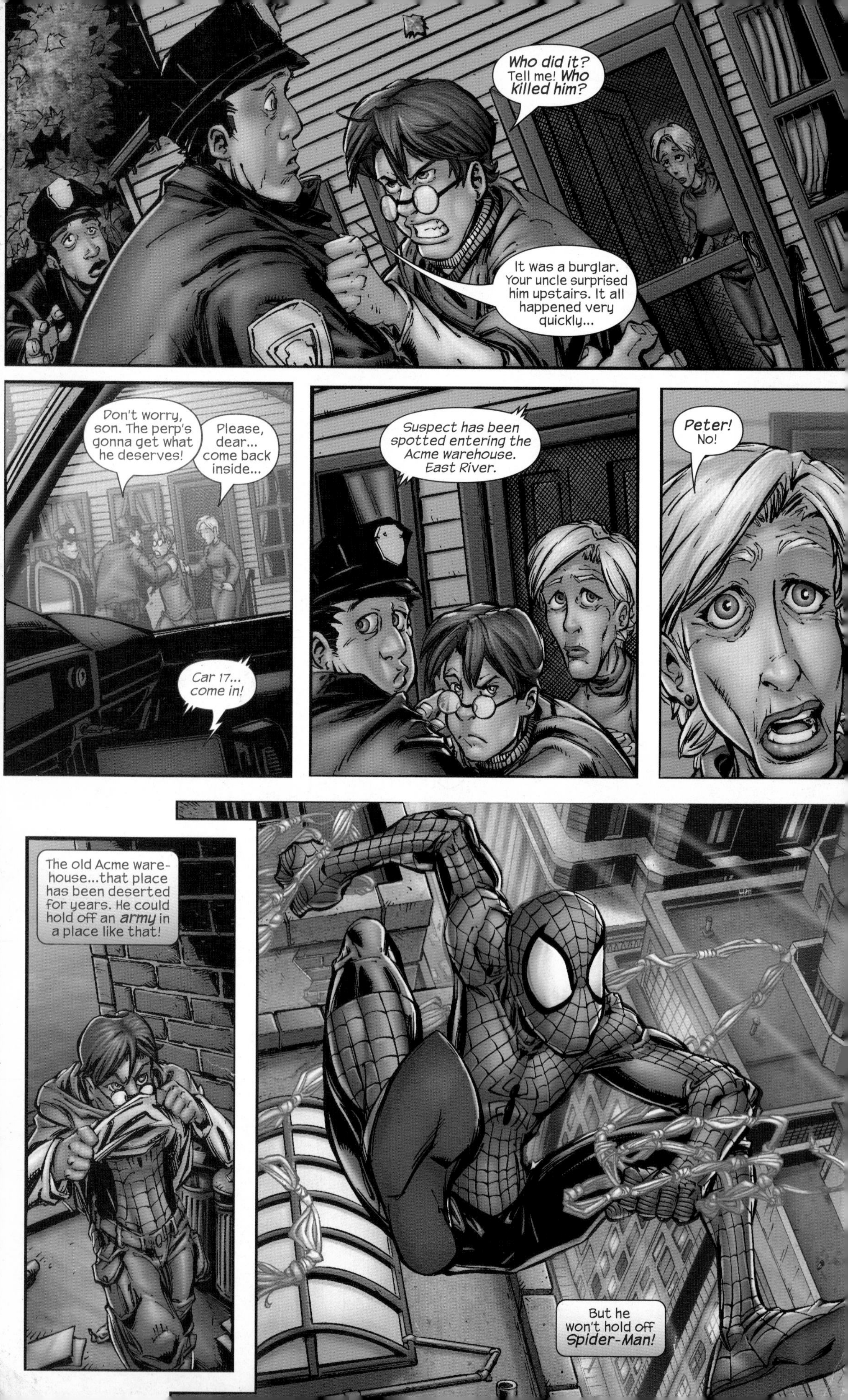
Who did it? Tell me! Who killed him?
It was a burglar. Your uncle surprised him upstairs. It all happened very quickly...
Don't worry, son. The perp's gonna get what he deserves!
Please, dear... come back inside...
Car 17... come in!
Suspect has been spotted entering the Acme warehouse. East River.
Peter! No!
The old Acme ware-house...that place has been deserted for years. He could hold off an army in a place like that!
But he won't hold off Spider-Man!

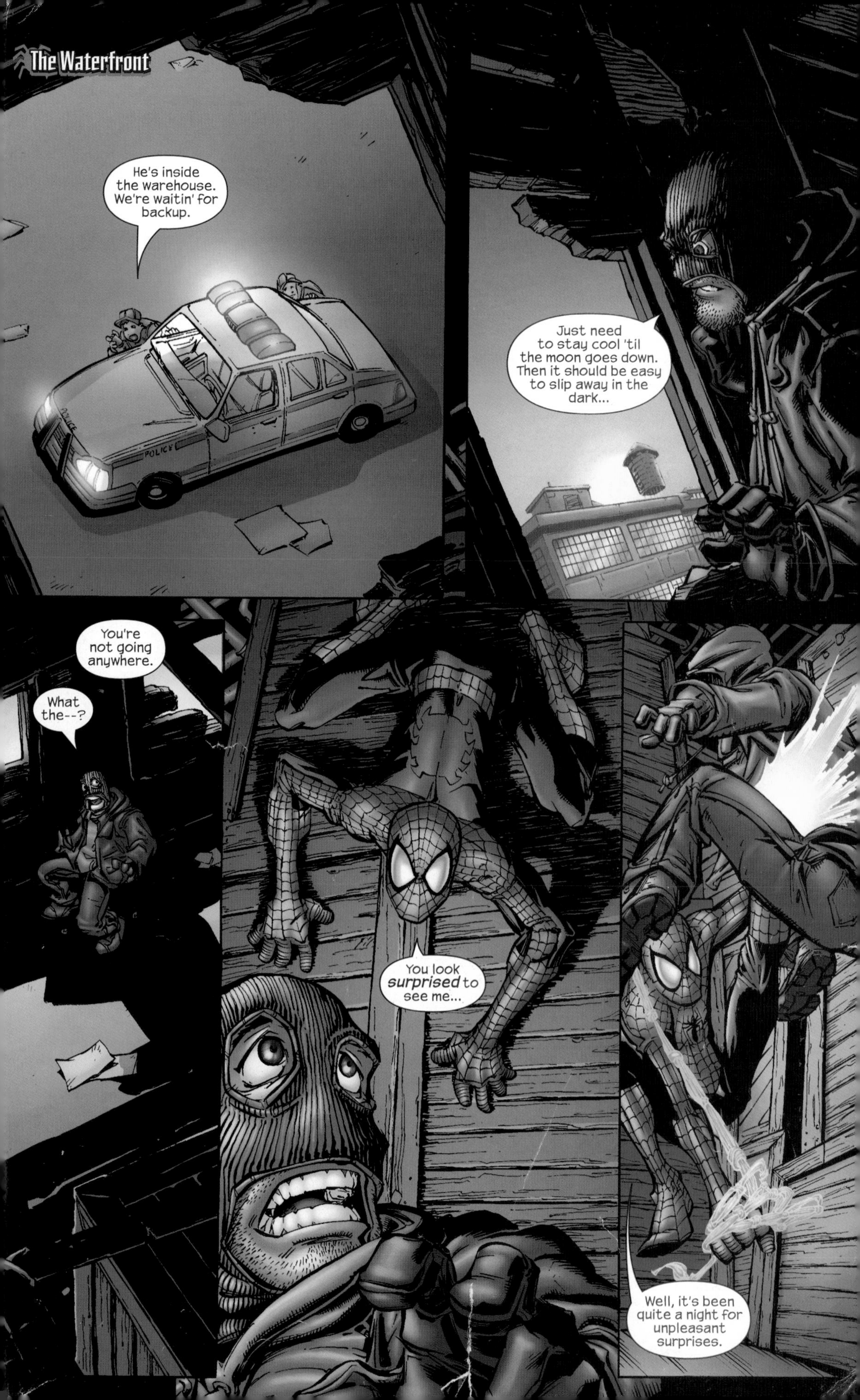
The Waterfront
He's inside the warehouse. We're waitin' for backup.
Just need to stay cool 'til the moon goes down. Then it should be easy to slip away in the dark...
You're not going anywhere.
What the--?
You look surprised to see me...
Well, it's been quite a night for unpleasant surprises.

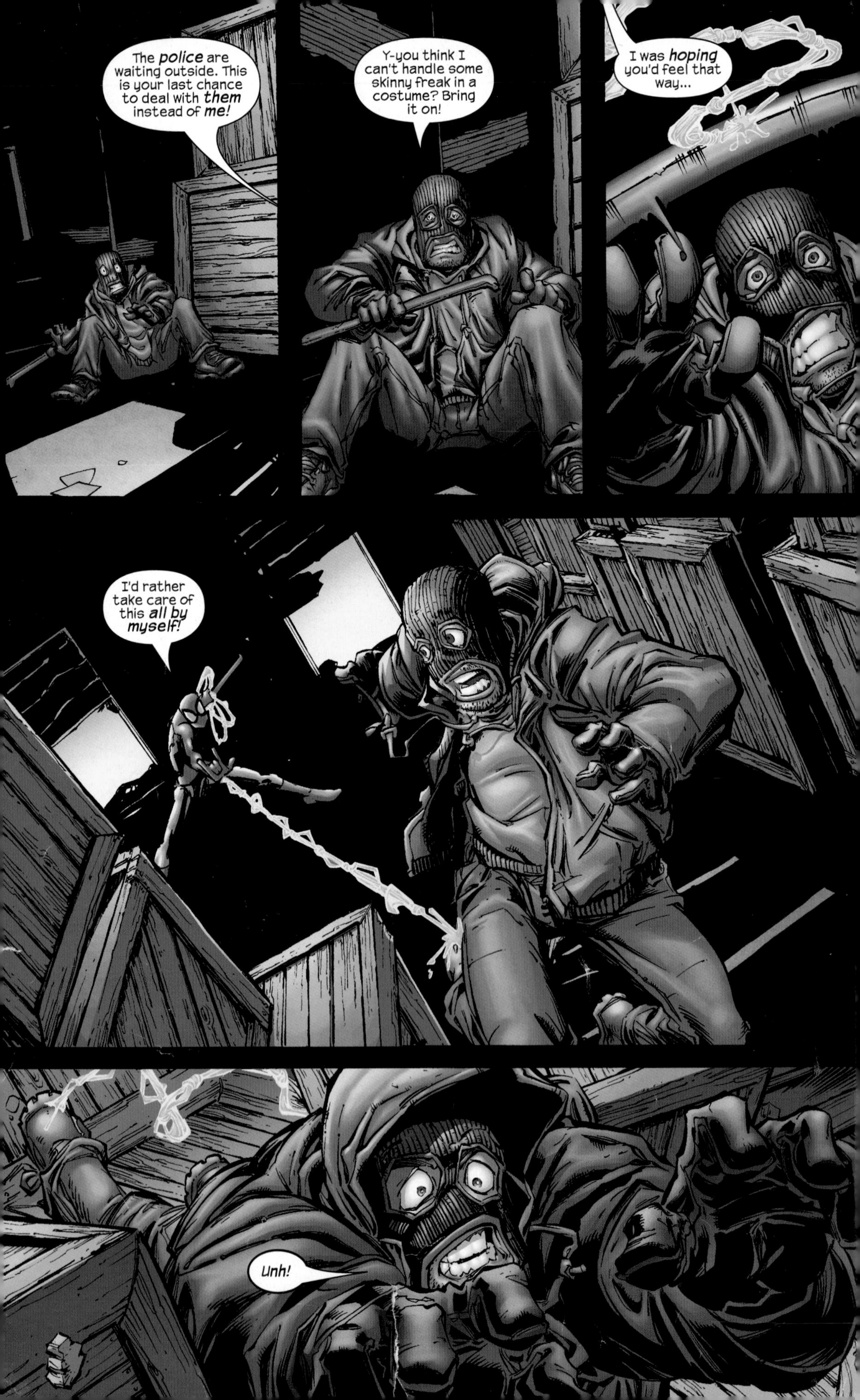
The police are waiting outside. This is your last chance to deal with them instead of me!
Y-you think I can't handle some skinny freak in a costume? Bring it on!
I was hoping you'd feel that way...
I'd rather take care of this all by myself!
Unh!

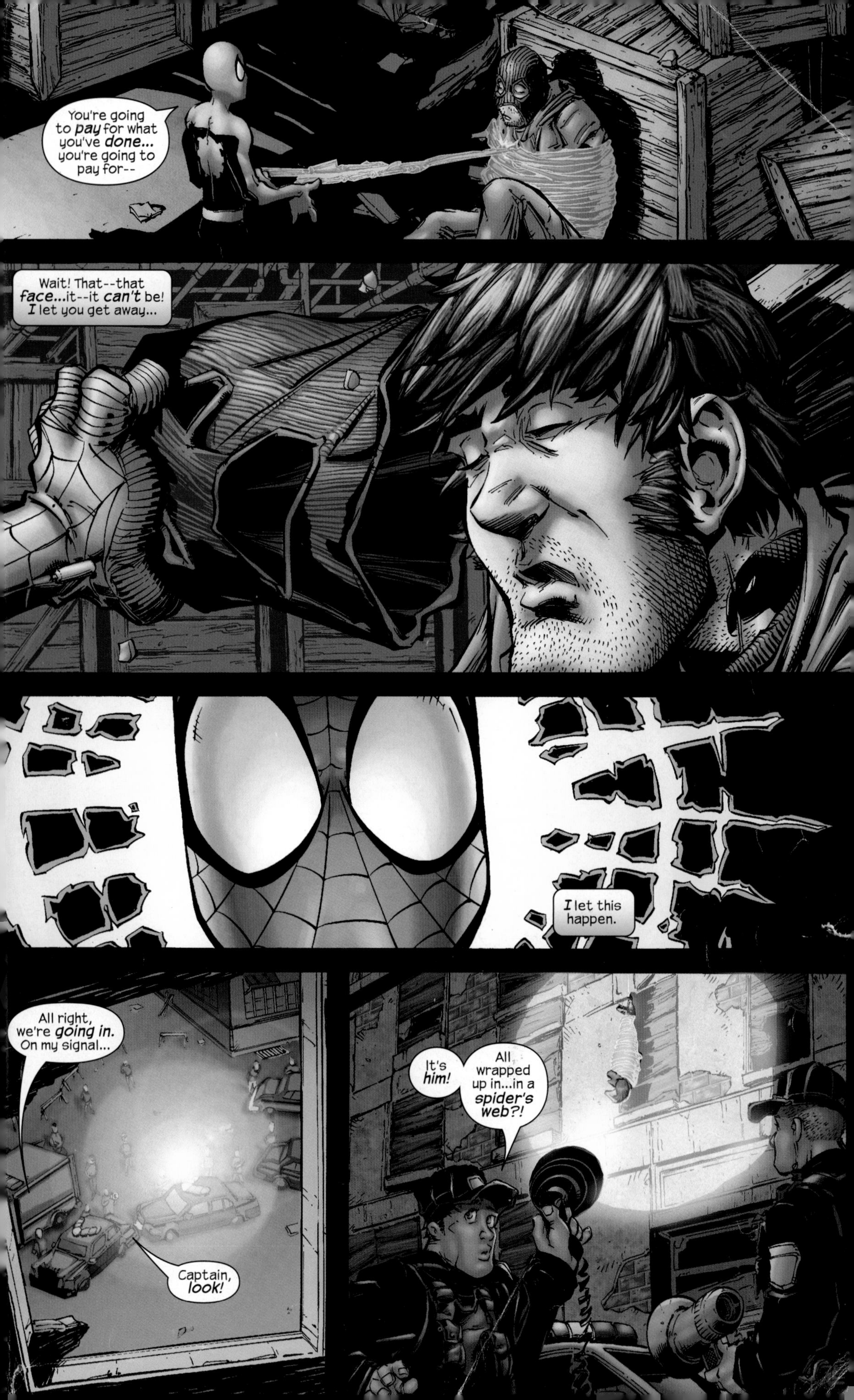
You're going to pay for what you've done... you're going to pay for--
Wait! That--that face...it--it can't be! I let you get away...
I let this happen.
All right, we're going in. On my signal...
Captain, look!
It's him!
All wrapped up in...in a spider's web?!

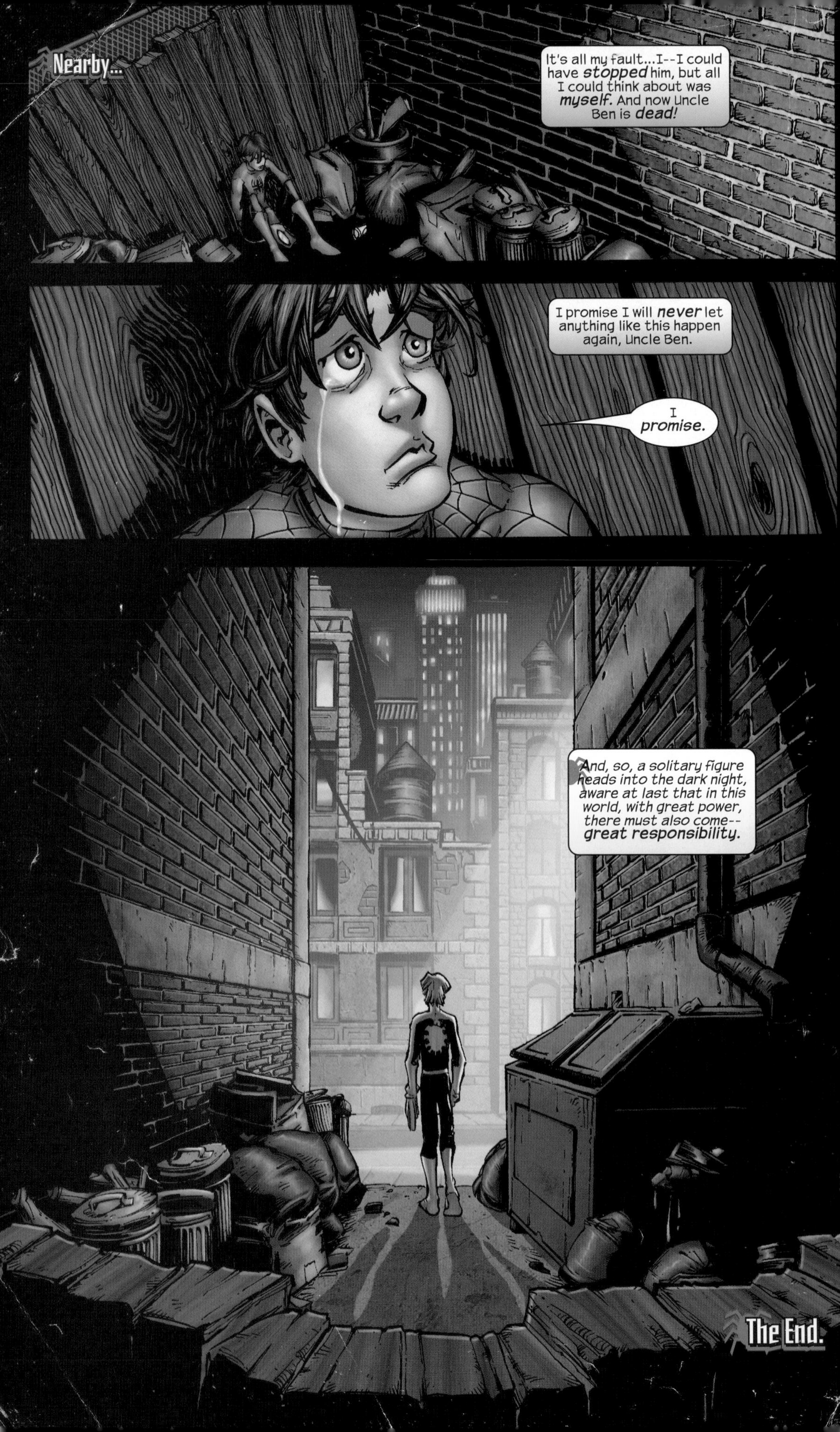
Nearby...
It's all my fault...I--I could have stopped him, but all I could think about was myself. And now Uncle Ben is dead!
I promise I will never let anything like this happen again, Uncle Ben.
I promise.
And, so, a solitary figure heads into the dark night, aware at last that in this world, with great power, there must also come--great responsibility.
The End.